Copyright © 2009 by NordSüd Verlag AG, CH-8005 Zürich, Switzerland.
First published in Switzerland under the title *Gut versteckt, kleiner Hase.*
English translation copyright © 2009 by North-South Books Inc., New York 10001.

First published in the United States, Great Britain, Canada, Australia,
and New Zealand in 2009 by North-South Books Inc., an imprint of NordSüd Verlag AG,
CH-8005 Zürich, Switzerland.
Distributed in the United States by North-South Books Inc., New York 10001.

Library of Congress Cataloging-in-Publication Data is available.
ISBN: 978-0-7358-2241-2 (trade edition)
10 9 8 7 6 5 4 3 2 1
Printed in China by SNP Leefung Packaging & Printing (Dongguan) Co., Ltd.,
Dongguan, P.R.C., October 2009

www.northsouth.com

Ernest's First Easter

by Päivi Stalder • illustrated by Frauke Weldin

NorthSouth
New York / London

It was Ernest's first Easter.

"We'll give you just one house to start with," said his dad. "Tommy's house. You can learn the ropes there."

"Take your time," said his mom. "Look for the perfect hiding place."

"Don't break the eggs," said his sister, Elsie.

Ernest had been preparing all week. He had marked Tommy's house with a big red X on his map. He had painted his eggs in brilliant colors. Then he had packed them up, ever so carefully. Ernest was ready!

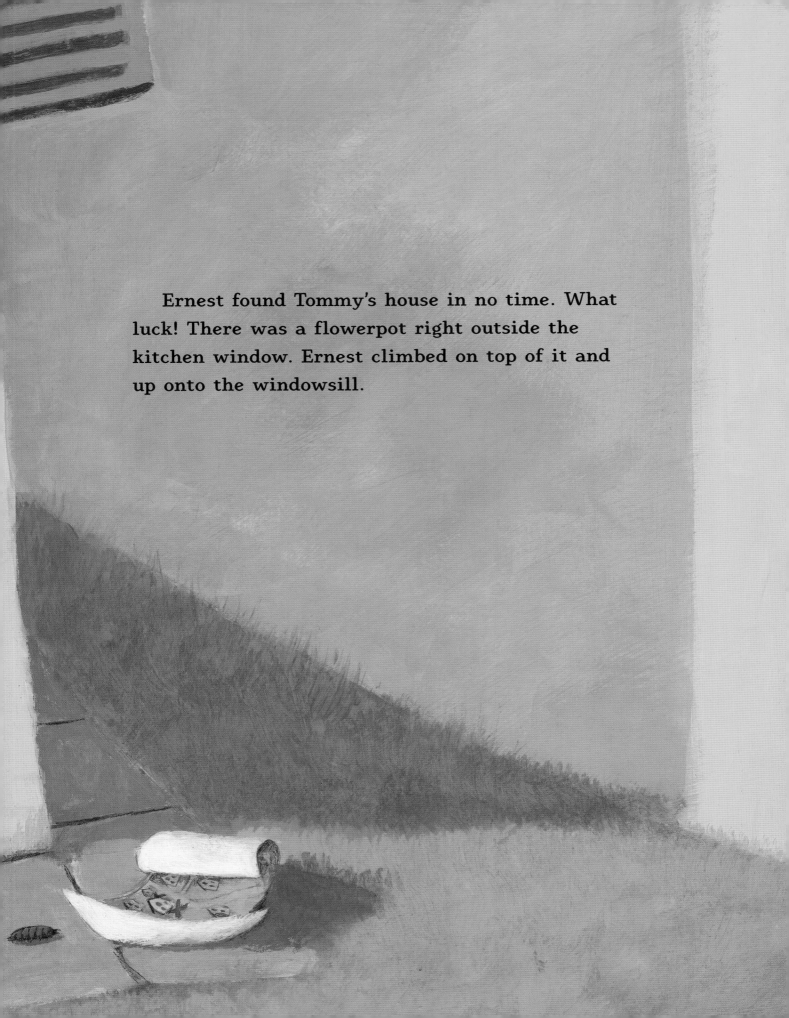

Ernest found Tommy's house in no time. What luck! There was a flowerpot right outside the kitchen window. Ernest climbed on top of it and up onto the windowsill.

CRASH! Oh, no! A flowerpot fell to the floor and broke into a hundred pieces.

Had it awoken anyone? Ernest held his breath. The house was silent.

Whew! That was a close call!

Tommy's room was just down the hall. Ernest slipped inside. Tommy was in his bed, sound asleep.

Now to find the perfect hiding place. In the fire truck? In the wastebasket? In the toy box?

Then Ernest spotted a basket with a pillow inside it. What could be more perfect? The eggs would be *really* safe there.

Suddenly, Ernest's whiskers started to tremble.
Someone was coming! Ernest dropped the eggs into
the basket and hid behind the toy box.

A nose poked through the doorway. A dog! He walked straight to the basket . . . and climbed in.

Oh, no! Ernest had hidden his eggs in the dog basket! What was he going to do now?

Ernest plucked up his courage. He hopped over to the dog basket.

"Excuse me," he said in a very polite whisper. "You are sitting on the Easter eggs."

The dog blinked. "Who are you?" he asked. "Are you new?"

"I'm Ernest," said Ernest. "And this is my very first Easter."

"I'm Fred," said the dog. "Thought you were new."

"Er . . . ," said Ernest. "The eggs?"

"Oh, yes," said Fred. "Let's check, shall we?"

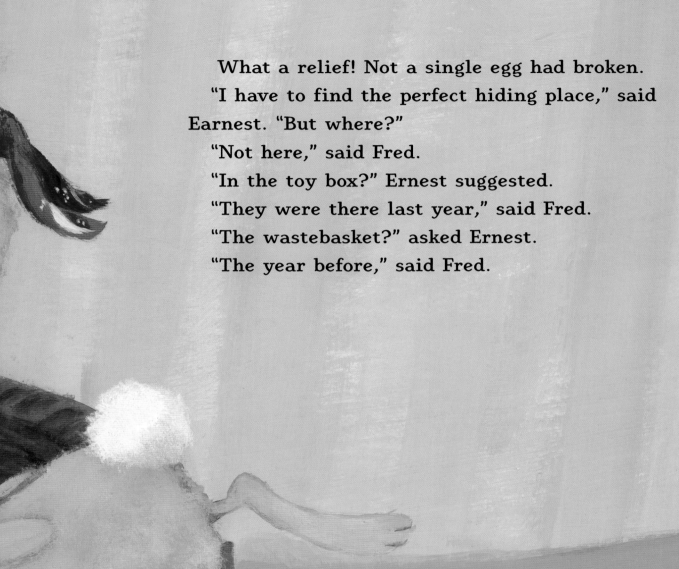

What a relief! Not a single egg had broken.

"I have to find the perfect hiding place," said Earnest. "But where?"

"Not here," said Fred.

"In the toy box?" Ernest suggested.

"They were there last year," said Fred.

"The wastebasket?" asked Ernest.

"The year before," said Fred.

"How about Tommy's backpack?" said Ernest.

"Been there too," said Fred.

This was harder than Ernest had expected.

"You can do it!" said Fred. "You new ones always find the best hiding places. Just keep looking."

Ernest looked all around the room. Then he looked again. And sure enough, there it was— the *perfect* hiding place!

"Good morning, Fred!" said Tommy as Ernest
scrambled out the window just in time. "Do you
know where the Easter Bunny left my eggs?"
Fred knew, all right, but Fred wasn't telling.

Tommy looked in the toy box. No eggs there.

He looked inside his fire truck. No eggs there either.

He emptied his wastebasket. No eggs.

He dumped out his backpack. Still no eggs.

"I think the Easter Bunny forgot me," said Tommy sadly.

Fred jumped out of his basket. It was time to give Tommy a hint.

There on the windowsill, tucked among Tommy's stuffed frog and donkey and dinosaur, were the beautiful Easter eggs.

"Oh, look!" cried Tommy. "The Easter Bunny *didn't* forget me. These are the best eggs ever! And what a great hiding place!"

Fred hurried outside to give Ernest the good news.
"You did it, Ernest!" he said. "You found the
perfect hiding place! Congratulations!"
"Thanks, Fred," said Ernest. "I couldn't have done
it without you! See you next year!"